Black Dan the Seventh

'The dog comes with the house,' the forester told us. 'If you want him.'

I looked at the dog. He was big and as black as night. He had soft, brown eyes, like a deer. And when I stroked him, he trembled all over.

'Please Dad, can we keep him?' I begged.

Mum, Dad, and me had just moved to our new house. It was a tiny cottage on the edge of a thick forest. My dad had a new job – as forest warden.

'No one said anything about a dog,' said Mum doubtfully. 'What kind of dog is it?'

'A racing greyhound,' said the forester. 'It belonged to Old Billy, who lived here before you. But he's in an old folk's home now.'

The dog trembled and looked up at me with his big, soft eyes.

'Please, Mum, please, Dad. Please, please, please –'

'Shut up a minute, Stevie.' Dad waved me to be quiet. Then he asked the forester: 'What'll happen to this dog if we don't take it?'

The forester shrugged. 'Well, I don't
know who else will want it. It's past its
best. It's not winning races any more.
Old Billy was going to get rid of it
anyway.'

The dog nuzzled his cold nose into
my hand.

'Dad, Dad,' I pleaded. I tugged at his
arm. 'I want this dog. I really, badly,
want him.'

Dad could see how frantic I was. 'All right, son,' he said. 'Calm down. But you've got to take him for walks, mind.'

'Of course I will! Thanks, Dad. You're a star, Dad!'

'He'll need lots of exercise,' said the forester.

He began to walk away, into the dark pine trees.

'Wait a minute!' I yelled after him. 'What's his name?'

'Black Dan!' he yelled back. 'He's Black Dan the Seventh. Old Billy had six greyhounds before him. And he called every one of them Black Dan.'

I hugged my dog round the neck.

'I won't get rid of you,' I told him. 'Just 'cos you don't win any more.'

And Black Dan whined and licked my hand.

Fiery eyes

That night, I couldn't get to sleep. The forest was making lots of weird noises. I hadn't noticed it before – how those trees creaked and rustled and groaned.

'Two-woooo!' An owl hooted.

'Is it always this spooky round here, Black Dan?'

He was curled up on my rug, trembling in his sleep.

Then I heard a new noise: 'Oow-oow-oow!' It sounded like a dog, howling.

Black Dan's ears started twitching like mad. Suddenly, his eyes shot open. He leaped up and ran to the bedroom door. He began scratching at it, frantic to get out. He was making little yelping noises.

'What's the matter? You don't want to go outside. It's cold and dark outside.'
I could feel the hairs on my neck doing Mexican waves.

There was more than one dog out
there! Other dogs were howling now:
'Oow-oow-oow!' Terrible, lonely howls
like children lost in the night and
crying for their mums.

I couldn't help shivering. My spine
felt like one big icicle. It was such a
creepy, lonely sound.

'Black Dan, can you hear that?'

He heard it all right. He went crazy!

His paws were raking at the wood. He was desperate to get out there, as if he wanted to join them. But I wasn't going to open the door.

'Go on, take a quick look out the window,' I dared myself. 'It's probably nothing.' I parted my bedroom curtains. Just a tiny crack.

The forest was like a dark, wild wood.
And looking out of it, from between the
trees, were six pairs of eyes. Red, fiery
eyes that stared towards my window.
They didn't move. They just stayed
there, glowing in the dark. As if they
were waiting for something...

I yanked the curtains shut.

'No, Black Dan, you're not going out there!'

I grabbed him. He struggled a bit. Then shivered and whimpered in my arms.

'You stay here with me,' I told him.

I didn't think I could fall asleep. I was too scared. But the next thing I knew it was morning. And I was waking up on the bedroom floor, cold and achy all over, with Black Dan nuzzling my hand.

'That dog should be dead'

At breakfast, Dad said: 'Stevie, why don't you take Black Dan for a run in the forest?'

But I said, 'I think he'll like it better in the fields.'

Then I said, 'Dad, are there lots of creatures in the forest? I looked out my window last night. I saw these eyes...'

Dad didn't seem surprised. He just shrugged. 'Could have been anything. Foxes, deer, rabbits, even owls. There's lots of wild creatures in the forest.'

I felt a bit better. I gave myself a good telling off. 'You wimp!' I told myself. 'Fancy being scared of six rabbits!'

A little voice in my head said: 'Rabbits don't have fiery eyes.'

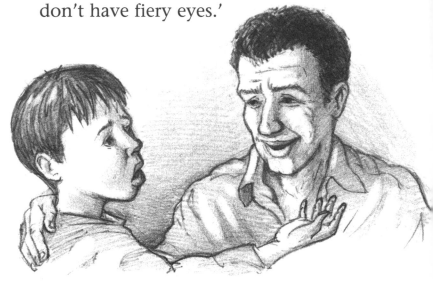

I said to Dad: 'Do rabbits howl? You know, like dogs do?'

He raised his eyebrows: 'Is that a *serious* question?'

16

After breakfast I called, 'Come on, boy,' to Black Dan.

As I was putting my coat on, Dad said, 'By the way, Stevie, if you do go in the forest, watch out for that old lead mine. Remember, I showed it to you? That tunnel with the iron grill over the front? Don't go in there. Right? Don't even think about it.'

I said: 'OK, Dad.'

I wasn't planning to go into the forest. No way. But it wasn't old lead mines I was scared of.

'Bye, Dad.'

Black Dan and I went running out of the house together.

Now, I'm not a wimp. I mean, not many things scare me. Except getting a whiskery kiss from my great-gran. Or the time I had to wear a frilly shirt and a velvet bow tie for my auntie's wedding. But I was scared that morning. You'd think daylight would make things less spooky. But that forest still looked grim and gloomy.

What was that? I jumped a mile. But it was just dark shadows trembling, under the pine trees.

'Come on,' I said, pulling on Black Dan's collar. 'You don't want to go in there.'

And we ran over the fields. Black Dan was a brilliant racer. He was so springy and quick. He ran so fast he was a blur! Then he jammed on the brakes. He made whippy turns, like you do on a skateboard.

'Black Dan, you're a star!' I yelled after
him.

I couldn't keep up with him, not if I'd
been the best runner in my school, the
world, the universe!

I started to run again. I was laughing
and panting, trying to keep up when,
blam! I ran straight into someone.

'Sorry! Sorry!'

It was the forester. He'd brought Black Dan to our house. But I still didn't like him much.

'Dog's running well,' he said, jerking his head towards Black Dan.

I mumbled something, just to be polite.

Then he laughed, a cruel sort of laugh. 'He had a lucky escape, that dog,' he said. 'The very day he was rushed to hospital, Old Billy was going to get rid of him.'

'What, you mean give him away?'

'No, get rid of him. Just like he did all his other Black Dans.'

'What did he do with them?'

'Well, it was like this. When Black Dan One stopped winning – that'd be when he was three or four years old – Old Billy took him off into the forest. He fed him poisoned meat.

'Then he bought Black Dan Two to replace him. Then when that dog started losing –'

He didn't have to go on. I'd got the picture. Six Black Dans all taken, one by one, into the forest. And my dog had almost been taken too.

'That dog should be dead by now,' said the forester, nodding at my Black Dan. 'It would have been, if Old Billy had had his way.'

That made me feel sick and shivery. All sorts of nightmare pictures came into my head.

I saw Old Billy, taking my Black Dan into the dark forest. And coming out alone.

And I saw those six pairs of red eyes, all staring out, as if they were waiting for something.

'Don't worry,' I said to my Black Dan. 'You're alive. Old Billy didn't take you into the forest. And now you're mine.'

And Black Dan trembled and huddled up close to me.

The howling

All that day I was dreading the night.
I kept telling myself: 'You saw rabbits
last night. You saw foxes or owls.'

I tried to believe it. By night-time I'd
nearly persuaded myself.

And, when I was in my bedroom with
Black Dan, I was even relaxing reading a
comic. Then –

'Oow-oow-oow!'

That howling started again.

Why couldn't Mum and Dad hear it?
There wasn't a sound from their
bedroom. It wasn't that late was it?
Surely they weren't asleep already?

Dan heard it. His ears went *flick, flick*.
And then he lifted his black head.
And started howling back.

The howls from the forest answered:
'Oow-oow-oow!'

It was such a dreary, lonesome sound.
Like the end of the world had come.

'Shut up, Black Dan. What are you making that awful noise for?'

Suddenly, before I could grab him, he nosed the door open and shot down the stairs.

'Stupid! You're stupid, Stevie!' I screamed at myself inside my head. 'You didn't shut the door properly!'

I went racing down after Black Dan.

My brain was like a scribble – I couldn't think straight. So I did another stupid thing. I looked around – couldn't see him. I thought, 'He must have got out somehow.' So I opened the front door!

What an idiot! He flew past me like an arrow. He was inside all the time!

He was heading straight for the forest. Somehow, I knew he would.

I was shaking now. Really panicking.
I didn't know what to do.

'Black Dan! Come back!'

But he didn't stop. He vanished into
the trees. And – oh no – I thought I saw
the flicker of fiery eyes! Then they
vanished too. Even the howling had
stopped. Everything was dark and silent.

'So what are you going to do now,
Stevie?' I asked myself.

Surrounded!

Of course I didn't have a choice, did I?
I had to go looking for him. I had to go
after my dog. And I knew by now what
that little voice in my head had been
telling me all day. That those eyes didn't
belong to owls or rabbits. Or even foxes.

Crunch, crunch. That was pine
needles under my feet. I walked towards
the forest and let it swallow me up.

It was pitch black inside. I could hear my own breathing. It sounded really loud.

What was that? Click, click, click. It was my teeth, chattering.

Then I heard it behind me. A very soft snarl, as if something was stalking me.

'Grrrr.'

I whipped round. 'Black Dan?' I whispered. 'Come 'ere boy.'

But there was no sign of my dog. No cold nose nuzzling my hand. I crept forwards.

A snarl came from another direction. 'Grrrr!'

Then another.

I was surrounded.

I could see red eyes and black greyhound shapes, creeping up on me.

I was frozen up – I couldn't move. But my mind was suddenly clear as an ice cube. I knew exactly what I'd walked into.

I'd walked into a pack of Black Dans. Ghost dogs in the forest. They'd been expecting my dog to join them. They'd been waiting for him to come.

I called my dog, 'Black Dan!' But I couldn't tell him from all the others.

I was shaking like I had rubber bones. But I got some strength from somewhere. I shouted into the dark.

'I know Billy was *going* to get rid of him. But he didn't get the chance. Right? So there's no point you lot hanging round any longer! He doesn't belong with you ghost dogs. He's not dead! He belongs with me!'

Tough words. But I didn't feel tough for long. Those ghostly Black Dans were closing in! I could see their white teeth! There! – no – there! They were all around!

I ran. Stupid thing, running. You can't outrun greyhounds. But I ran anyway, bashing into bushes, falling down, staggering to my feet, running on.

The old mine

Then, *clang*, I crashed into an iron grill.
I bashed it so hard that it fell over. At
last, I knew where I was.

'The old mine!' my scrambled brain
told me. The grill had been propped up,
over the entrance.

'Get in!' my brain screamed at me.
'Hide! Hide! Get inside!'

I ran into the tunnel.

Straight away I was in pitch blackness.
Something brushed at my face.

'Gerroff!'

Frantic, I brushed it away. But it was
only ferns, growing in the tunnel
entrance. I listened. I couldn't hear
anything. Except my own heart
thudding away. And the drip, drip, drip
of water on the mine walls.

I stumbled a few steps along the tunnel.

Then Dad's warnings flashed into my head. 'That old lead mine is a death-trap. You're walking along the tunnel. You think you're OK. Then suddenly there's a deep shaft right under your feet. If you fall into that, you could be falling for half a mile!'

'Just stay here,' I told myself, huddling against the slimy walls. 'Don't go any further in. You'll be all right. If you just stay here.'

And I would have been all right. Only I saw something, back at the mine entrance. What was it? I could feel my skin crawling. There were red eyes, burning in the darkness – the pack of Black Dans. They'd found me, sniffed me out. And they were coming into the mine to get me.

Panic took over. I just ran like a
hunted animal. I ran deeper into the
mine. I didn't care, anything to get
away.

Then a rock tripped me up. Wham!
I went crashing down.

'Oh, no! Get off me.
Oh, no!'

My yells echoed up and down the tunnel. One of them had got me! I could feel its teeth, tugging at my jeans. It tried to drag me backwards. I crawled the other way, scrabbling at the rocks with my hands. Then suddenly, my hands were clutching at thin air! There was empty space where the tunnel floor should be. I was on the very edge of a mine shaft.

Then a cold nose nuzzled my face.

'Black Dan! Good boy, good boy!' I was sobbing with relief.

He'd dragged me back, stopped me from falling down the shaft. He'd saved my life.

I pulled myself away from the edge. A rock went clattering into the shaft. It seemed a long, long, long time before it hit the bottom.

Then I heard another sound.

'Grrrr!'

The others were coming. They had me cornered. I had nowhere to go. Nowhere to hide. I tried to get up. A hot pain shot through my leg. I just crouched there, watching their red eyes come nearer, nearer.

I could see their slinky shapes, blacker
than blackness, sliding down the tunnel
towards me.

Black Dan was trembling by my side.
He whined.

'Shhh, boy.'

They were here. They knew I was
wounded. They darted in to attack.

They came rushing in – eyes blazing,
teeth snapping. I rolled into a ball like a
hedgehog and covered my head with
my hands. I thought, 'They've got me
now.'

Suddenly, another dog was barking. Standing by my side, protecting me and barking into the dark. He sounded fierce and brave as a lion. It was the seventh Black Dan. My Black Dan.

He was scaring off the other six! Those barks meant: 'Clear off, you ghost dogs! I don't belong with you! I belong here with Stevie!'

Black Dan stopped barking.

Silence. All I could hear was dripping water.

I unrolled myself, very slowly. And peered past my Black Dan into the darkness beyond.

The ghost pack was still there.

For a few seconds they watched us.
But they didn't come any closer. Then,
one by one, they sort of shrivelled away.
Their burning eyes shrunk to red
pinpricks. Then they just vanished, like
genies sucked back into a bottle.

'They've gone!' I told Black Dan. 'You
brave dog. You hero!'

When I tried to get up I went, 'Ouch!' and nearly fell down again. I had to lean on Black Dan. And, somehow, together, we made it out of that mine.

In the forest I made a crutch out of a branch and I limped back home, with faithful Black Dan guarding me all the way.

In the forest

Next morning Mum said, 'Stevie, have you got a bad leg?'

'What, me? Of course I haven't,' I said, trying not to wince.

And I limped out of the door with Black Dan.

'I won't be able to run in the fields with you today,' I told him.

But he wasn't heading towards the fields. He was heading for the forest!

Straight away, my stomach clenched up tight.

I limped after him yelling, 'No, Black Dan, don't go in there. Stay with me!'

Too late. He slipped like a ghost into the forest. I went after him, hobbling as fast as I could, crashing through branches, calling his name, 'Black Dan! Black Dan!'

I felt sick with despair. I'd really believed he'd chosen to stay with me. I'd really believed it.

Then I stopped.

'Black Dan, there you are!'

He came quietly to my side and nuzzled my hand.

I looked about me. We were in a forest clearing. Little birds were twittering. Sunlight was dancing all around us. And, you know what? That forest didn't feel spooky or dangerous at all.

It felt like our forest. It felt like those ghost dogs had given up waiting and left it for good.

I never told Dad or Mum what happened.

I mean, how could I even start? I'd get out a few words: 'There was this pack of six ghostly Black Dans –'

And they'd say: 'Is this supposed to be *serious*?' Well, what would you say?

About the author

I live in County Durham.
One day I was walking
round the 'back lanes'
with my three children
when we met an old man
with his racing
greyhound. My son said,
'What's his name?' And
the old man said, 'He's

called Black Dan. All my racing dogs
are called Black Dan.' And that set me thinking.
I don't quite know how I ended up writing this
ghost story, just from that tiny snippet of
conversation in a back lane. But imagination is
a wonderful thing!